Jean Van Leeuwen

SORRY

pictures by Brad Sneed

Phyllis Fogelman Books
New York

Published by Phyllis Fogelman Books
An imprint of Penguin Putnam Books for Young Readers
345 Hudson Street
New York, New York 10014

Designed by Nancy R. Leo-Kelly
Text set in Meridien
Printed in Hong Kong on acid-free paper
1 3 5 7 9 10 8 6 4 2

Library of Congress Cataloging-in-Publication Data
Van Leeuwen, Jean.
Sorry/by Jean Van Leeuwen; pictures by Brad Sneed.—1st ed.
p. cm.
Summary: Two brothers who cannot apologize to each other extend their feud down through their children, grandchildren, and great-grandchildren.
ISBN 0-8037-2261-3
[1. Brothers—Fiction. 2. Obstinacy—Fiction. 3. Behavior—Fiction.]
I. Sneed, Brad, ill. II. Title.
PZ7.V275 So 2001 [E]—dc21 00-026852

The paintings for this book were created with watercolor on 140-pound cold-pressed watercolor paper.

To Bruce —J.V.L.

To my teachers —B.S.

In a little house perched on a hilltop, high in the mountains of north country, lived two brothers. Ebenezer and Obadiah, their names were. Ebenezer was tall as a long drink of spring water. Obadiah was lean as a pitchfork. They lived together on a poor farm with more rocks than good soil, more winter than summer sun.

Ebenezer cooked. Obadiah cleaned. Ebenezer walked behind Nelly, the old gray mare, as she pulled the plow. Obadiah milked Bertha, the cow. And in the evenings they both sat on the porch playing tunes—Ebenezer on his fiddle, Obadiah on his mouth organ—till the sun went down.

One morning, when winter had been hanging on so long it looked like it would never let go, Ebenezer cooked up a nice hot pot of oatmeal.

"Snowed again," he said.

"Yep," said Obadiah.

The brothers never did talk much.

They ate awhile.

"Lumps," said Obadiah.

"Lumps?" said Ebenezer. "Not in my oatmeal."

"Lumps," said Obadiah.

Something came over Ebenezer then: too much winter or too much pride. He picked up Obadiah's bowl and turned it over on his brother's head.

Obadiah was so surprised, he just sat there with the bowl on his head like a hat, oatmeal dripping down.

All that day the brothers didn't talk at all. Ebenezer was waiting for Obadiah to say he was sorry. Obadiah was waiting for Ebenezer to say *he* was sorry. Ebenezer cooked for himself. Obadiah tried to cook for himself. He burned everything. Still, neither one said a word.

Silence hung over the little house like a heavy, wet coat.

Days crawled by. Ebenezer noticed that Obadiah never picked up his socks. Obadiah noticed that Ebenezer had a bothersome way of whistling out of tune. It got so they couldn't bear to look at each other. Obadiah moved to one end of the house. Ebenezer stayed in the other.

Still, they sometimes met in the kitchen.

One day, when the snow had finally turned to mud and leaves were popping out green on the trees, Ebenezer heard the buzz of a saw. Looking out, he saw Obadiah cutting the house in two.

"Stop!" he wanted to shout. "I'm sorry." But he didn't.

Obadiah hauled away his half of the house, along with Bertha, the milk cow. He set them down on the next hilltop.

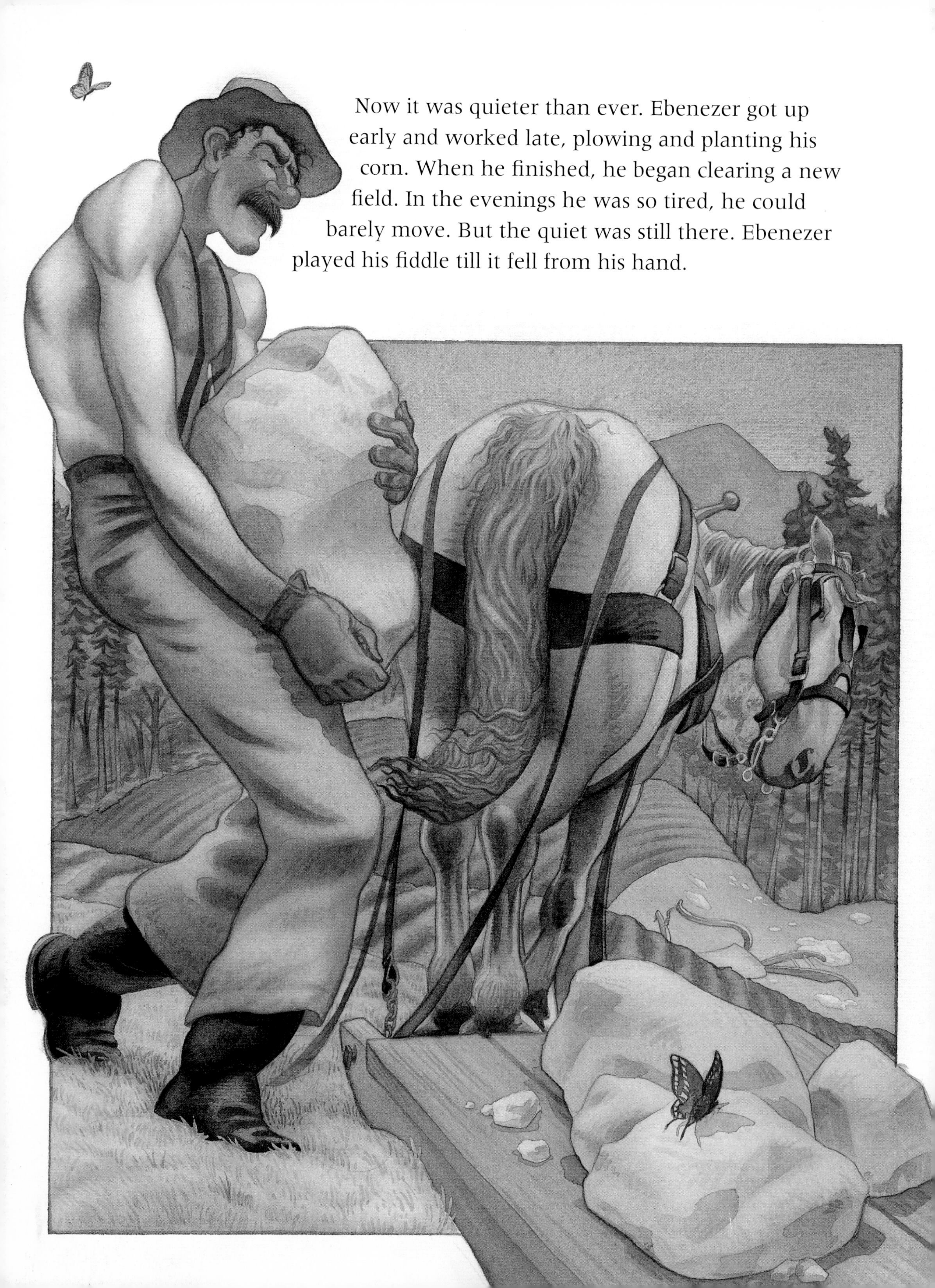

Now it was quieter than ever. Ebenezer got up early and worked late, plowing and planting his corn. When he finished, he began clearing a new field. In the evenings he was so tired, he could barely move. But the quiet was still there. Ebenezer played his fiddle till it fell from his hand.

Obadiah felt the quiet too. He got so he talked to Bertha while he milked her. She gave so much milk that he started selling it in town. Pretty soon he bought another cow. And another. They needed a barn, so Obadiah got busy building. But in the evenings he had to go inside where the quiet was. Obadiah played his mouth organ till he ran out of tunes.

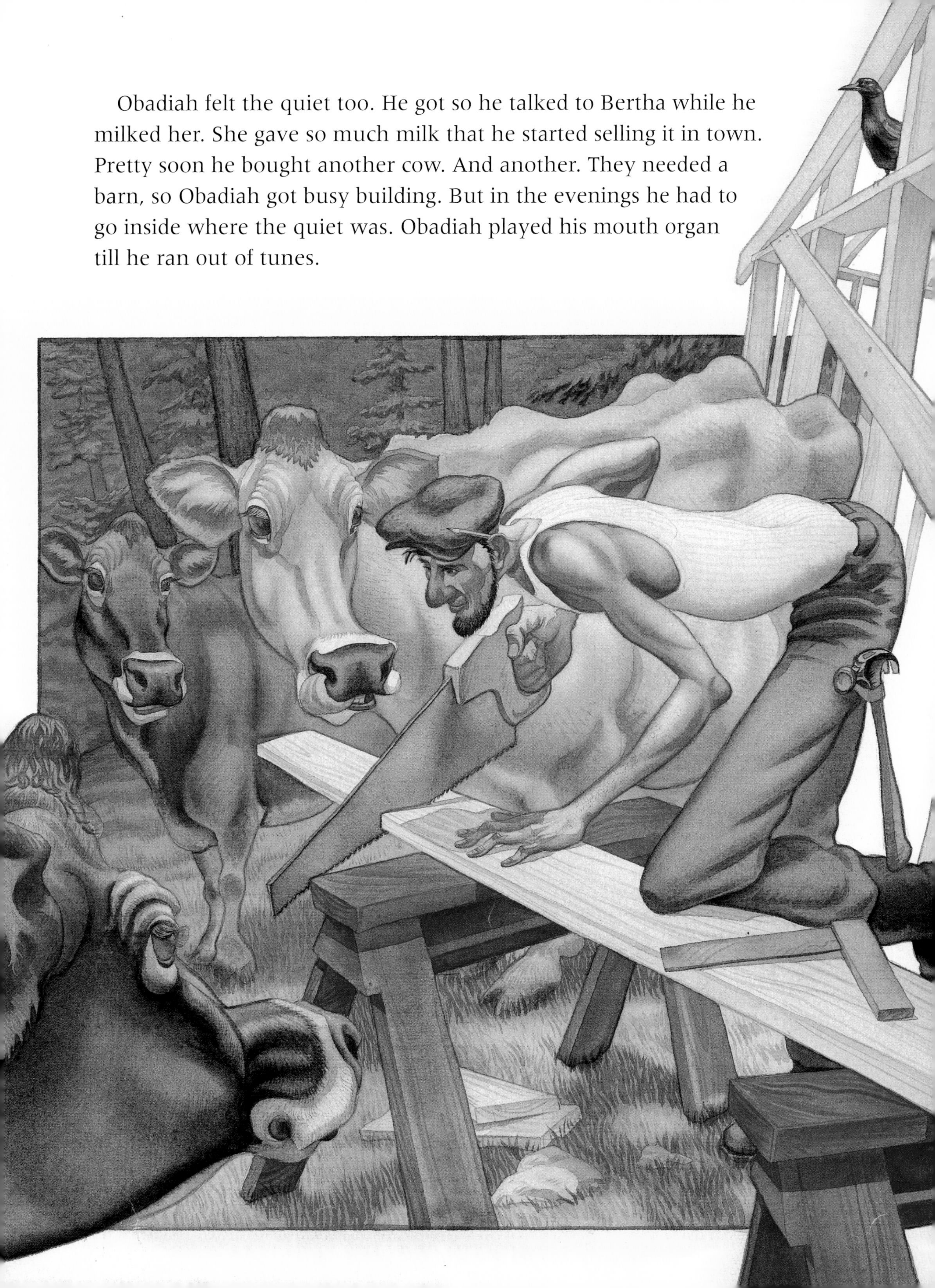

Sometimes, when the breeze was just right, the brothers could hear each other playing.

They were sad and lonesome sounds.

A year passed. Ebenezer kept clearing more fields and planting more corn. Obadiah kept selling more milk and buying more cows. His cows

liked to wander, and once in a while they got into Ebenezer's corn. So Ebenezer piled up rocks till he had built a wall to keep them out.

At harvest time he took his corn to the mill.
"Howdy-do," said the miller.
He was the first person Ebenezer had talked to in over a year. All afternoon he sat in the shade and talked to the miller and his daughter. Her name was Susannah and she had hair like corn silk.

In the spring Ebenezer and Susannah were married.

Soon after that, Obadiah got tired of talking to his cows, who never talked back, and spoke to Abigail, the schoolmistress. Her soft brown eyes reminded him of Bertha's, but he didn't tell her that. By fall they were married.

With their wives to help, the brothers' farms prospered. Ebenezer's corn fields spread uphill and down. And Obadiah had the largest, most contented herd of cows in all of north country.

Ebenezer built his wall longer and stouter to keep them out.

When his first son was born, Ebenezer was fit to bust his buttons with pride. He wanted to shout the news to Obadiah: "Caleb is here!" But then he remembered. He took down his fiddle and played the most rollicking, joyful tune. Over on his hilltop Obadiah heard it, and he knew.

Before long he had a baby girl of his own. To celebrate, Obadiah planted an apple tree right next to Ebenezer's wall. When the wind rustled the leaves, they seemed to say "Sophie is here." In his cornfield Ebenezer heard it, and he knew.

The years marched by. Ebenezer had six strapping sons. Obadiah had five daughters with soft brown eyes. And a whole orchard of apple trees.

Sometimes the brothers passed each other on the way to town. But they never spoke.

"Why?" asked Caleb when he was old enough to wonder.

"Lumps" was all his father would say.

Caleb and his brothers puzzled over that long and hard. Lumps of coal? Lumps on the head, like goose eggs? It had to be something terrible. No doubt about it, Uncle Obadiah was a bad man.

"Upside down on my head." Sophie and her sisters wondered what that could mean. Upside down in a snowdrift? Upside down in the pigpen? It had to be something dreadful. No doubt about it, Uncle Ebenezer was a mean man.

Caleb and his brothers built the wall longer. It snaked uphill and down, making each farm look like a fortress.

Generations passed. Ebenezer and Obadiah had grandchildren, then great-grandchildren. No one in either family ever spoke to the other, though they couldn't quite remember why. Rumor had it that Obadiah had stolen Ebenezer's cows. Or maybe Ebenezer had cheated Obadiah out of his land.

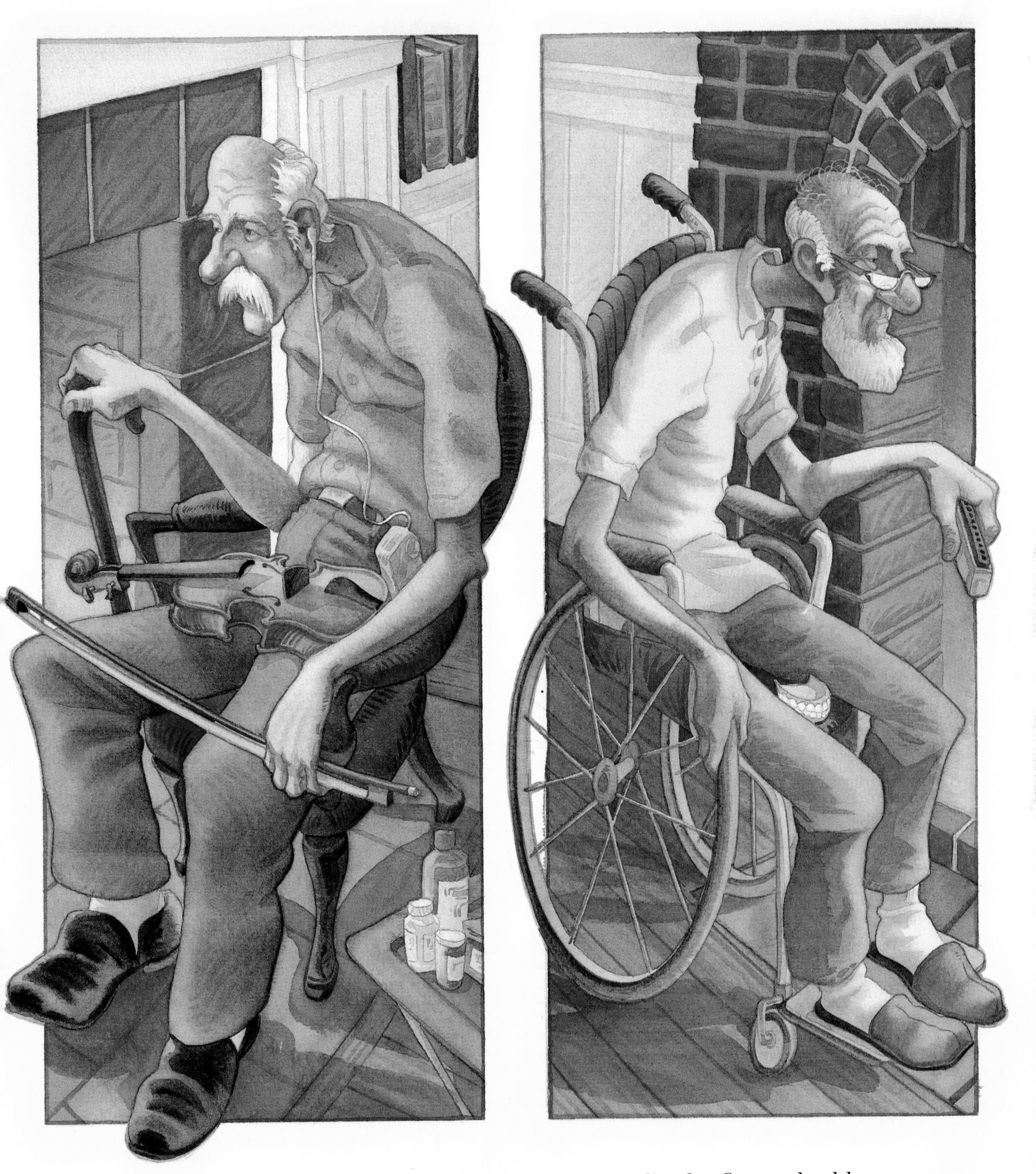

The brothers were very old men now. They sat by the fire and seldom said a word. Now and then Ebenezer would pick up his fiddle or Obadiah his mouth organ. But they played too softly to be heard on the next hilltop.

One summer day a boy named Nathaniel, Ebenezer's great-grandson, was sent to inspect the wall between the farms. "Something's been getting into our corn," his father said. "Must be those fool cows."

The very same day a boy named Luther, Obadiah's great-grandson, was sent to look over the wall. "Somebody's been helping themselves to our apples," his mother said. "We've only been able to pick twelve bushels this year."

Nathaniel looked, but he couldn't find anything wrong. As he sat down

to rest, something fell out of the sky right into his hand. It was an apple.

He was about to take a bite when a voice said, "That's my apple."

On the other side of the wall, scowling at him, was a boy.

"So you're the one been stealing our apples," said the boy.

"Must be you're the one getting into our corn," answered Nathaniel.

They stood staring and glaring and doubling up their fists. Isn't this just like that miserable old Ebenezer? Luther was thinking. What can you expect from that ornery old Obadiah? Nathaniel was thinking.

Something came over Nathaniel then: all that warm summer sun or all that loneliness. He did a most peculiar thing.

"Sorry," he said.

Luther just stared. He couldn't figure out what to say. He opened his mouth and all that came out was a smile.

“We maybe could trade,” he said when he recovered himself. “Some of your corn for some of my apples.”

“We maybe could,” said Nathaniel.

The two boys—cousins they were—sat side by side on the stone wall with their feet dangling down. And they talked and ate apples and laughed till the sun went down.

DATE